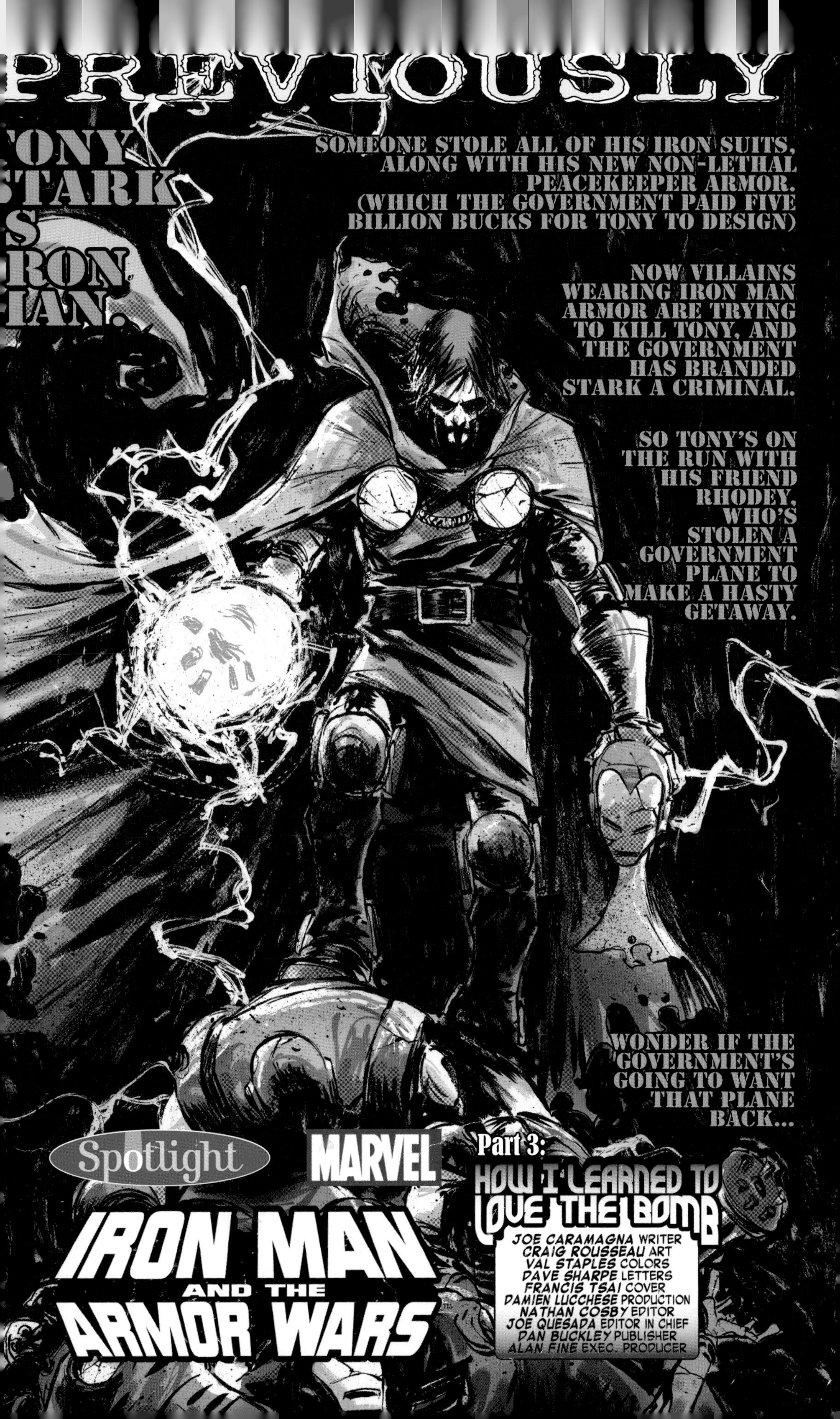
PREVIOUSLY
TONY STARK S RON IAN.
SOMEONE STOLE ALL OF HIS IRON SUITS, ALONG WITH HIS NEW NON-LETHAL PEACEKEEPER ARMOR. (WHICH THE GOVERNMENT PAID FIVE BILLION BUCKS FOR TONY TO DESIGN)
NOW VILLAINS WEARING IRON MAN ARMOR ARE TRYING TO KILL TONY, AND THE GOVERNMENT HAS BRANDED STARK A CRIMINAL.
SO TONY'S ON THE RUN WITH HIS FRIEND RHODEY, WHO'S STOLEN A GOVERNMENT PLANE TO MAKE A HASTY GETAWAY.
WONDER IF THE GOVERNMENT'S GOING TO WANT THAT PLANE BACK...
Spotlight
MARVEL
Part 3:
HOW I LEARNED TO LOVE THE BOMB
IRON MAN AND THE ARMOR WARS
JOE CARAMAGNA WRITER
CRAIG ROUSSEAU ART
VAL STAPLES COLORS
DAVE SHARPE LETTERS
FRANCIS TSAI COVER
DAMIEN LUCCHESE PRODUCTION
NATHAN COSBY EDITOR
JOE QUESADA EDITOR IN CHIEF
DAN BUCKLEY PUBLISHER
ALAN FINE EXEC. PRODUCER

Visit us at www.abdopublishing.com

Reinforced library bound editions published in 2014 by Spotlight, a division of the ABDO Group, PO Box 398166, Minneapolis, MN 55439. Spotlight produces high-quality reinforced library bound editions for schools and libraries. Published by agreement with Marvel Characters, Inc.

Printed in the United States of America, Melrose Park, Illinois.
042013
012014
♻ This book contains at least 10% recycled material.

marvel.com
© 2013 Marvel

Library of Congress Cataloging-in-Publication Data

Caramagna, Joe.
  Iron Man and the armor wars / story by Joe Caramagna ; art by Craig Rousseau. -- Reinforced library edition.
       volumes cm
  Summary: "Cash, cars, boats, houses...Tony Stark has got it all. The only thing that could ruin his day? If every single one of his Iron Man armors were stolen, and then turned against him"-- Provided by publisher.
  ISBN 978-1-61479-164-5 (part 1: Down and out in Beverly Hills) --
  ISBN 978-1-61479-165-2 (part 2: The big red machine) --
  ISBN 978-1-61479-166-9 (part 3: How I learned to love the bomb) --
  ISBN 978-1-61479-167-6 (part 4: The Golden Avenger strikes back)
  1. Graphic novels. I. Rousseau, Craig, illustrator. II. Title.
  PZ7.7.C3653Iro 2013
  741.5'3--dc23
                              2013003434

All Spotlight books are reinforced library bindings
and manufactured in the United States of America.

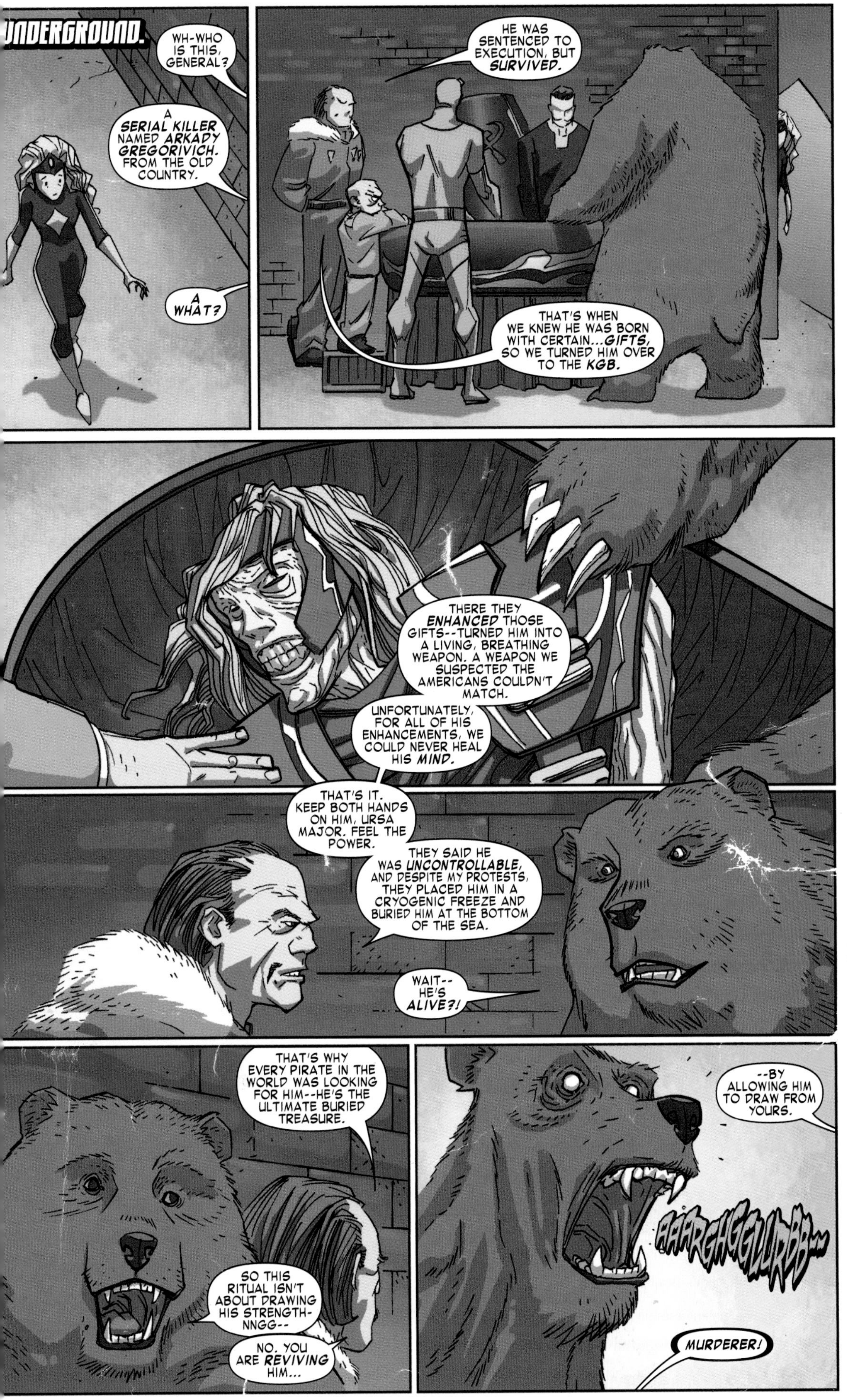
UNDERGROUND.
WH-WHO IS THIS, GENERAL?
A SERIAL KILLER NAMED ARKADY GREGORIVICH. FROM THE OLD COUNTRY.
A WHAT?
HE WAS SENTENCED TO EXECUTION, BUT SURVIVED.
THAT'S WHEN WE KNEW HE WAS BORN WITH CERTAIN...GIFTS, SO WE TURNED HIM OVER TO THE KGB.
THERE THEY ENHANCED THOSE GIFTS--TURNED HIM INTO A LIVING, BREATHING WEAPON. A WEAPON WE SUSPECTED THE AMERICANS COULDN'T MATCH.
UNFORTUNATELY, FOR ALL OF HIS ENHANCEMENTS, WE COULD NEVER HEAL HIS MIND.
THAT'S IT. KEEP BOTH HANDS ON HIM, URSA MAJOR. FEEL THE POWER.
THEY SAID HE WAS UNCONTROLLABLE, AND DESPITE MY PROTESTS, THEY PLACED HIM IN A CRYOGENIC FREEZE AND BURIED HIM AT THE BOTTOM OF THE SEA.
WAIT-- HE'S ALIVE?!
THAT'S WHY EVERY PIRATE IN THE WORLD WAS LOOKING FOR HIM--HE'S THE ULTIMATE BURIED TREASURE.
SO THIS RITUAL ISN'T ABOUT DRAWING HIS STRENGTH-NNGG--
NO. YOU ARE REVIVING HIM...
--BY ALLOWING HIM TO DRAW FROM YOURS.
AAARGHGGLURBB...
MURDERER!

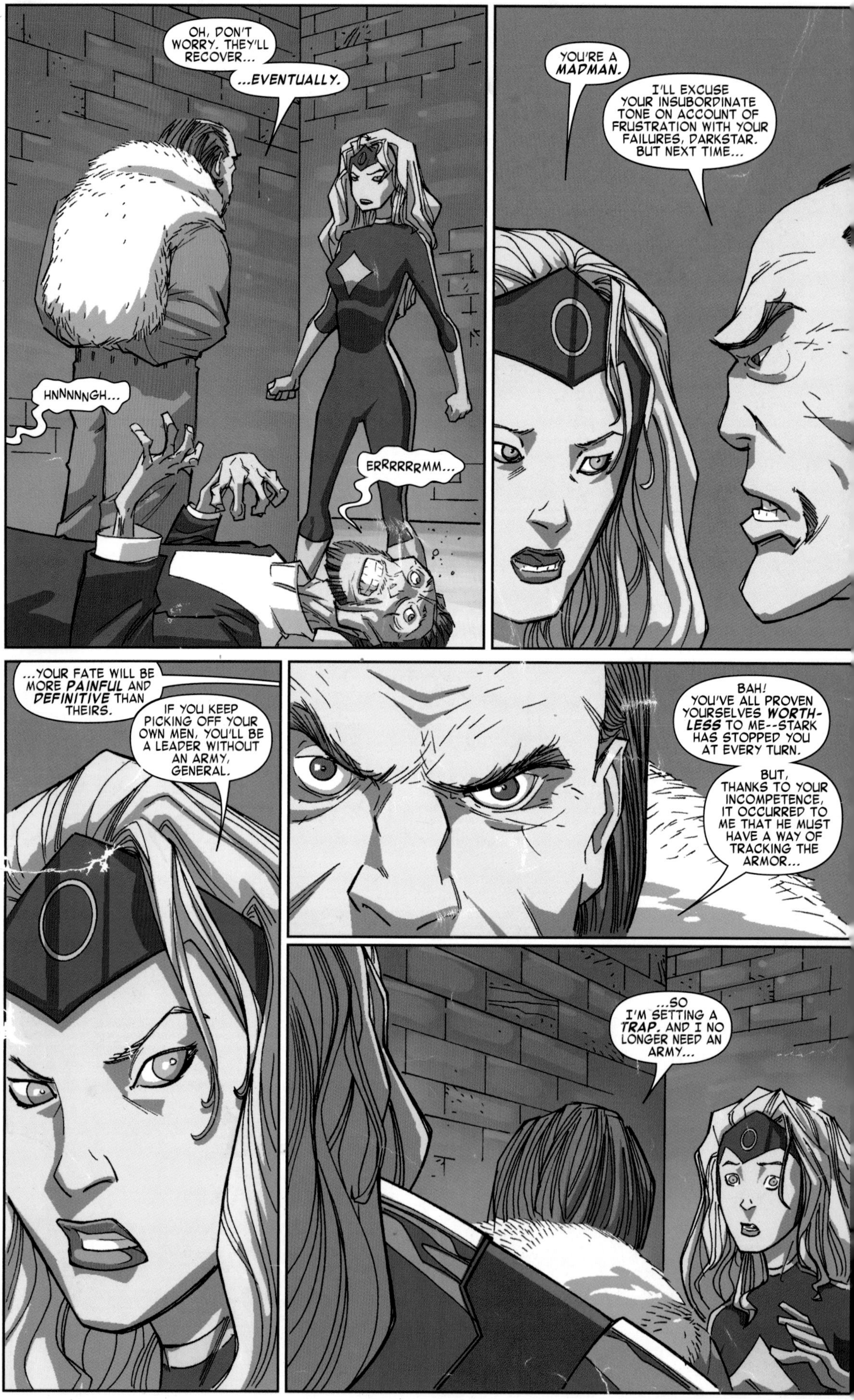
OH, DON'T WORRY. THEY'LL RECOVER...
...EVENTUALLY.
HNNNNNGH...
ERRRRRRMM...
YOU'RE A MADMAN.
I'LL EXCUSE YOUR INSUBORDINATE TONE ON ACCOUNT OF FRUSTRATION WITH YOUR FAILURES, DARKSTAR. BUT NEXT TIME...
...YOUR FATE WILL BE MORE PAINFUL AND DEFINITIVE THAN THEIRS.
IF YOU KEEP PICKING OFF YOUR OWN MEN, YOU'LL BE A LEADER WITHOUT AN ARMY, GENERAL.
BAH! YOU'VE ALL PROVEN YOURSELVES WORTHLESS TO ME--STARK HAS STOPPED YOU AT EVERY TURN.
BUT, THANKS TO YOUR INCOMPETENCE, IT OCCURRED TO ME THAT HE MUST HAVE A WAY OF TRACKING THE ARMOR...
...SO I'M SETTING A TRAP. AND I NO LONGER NEED AN ARMY...

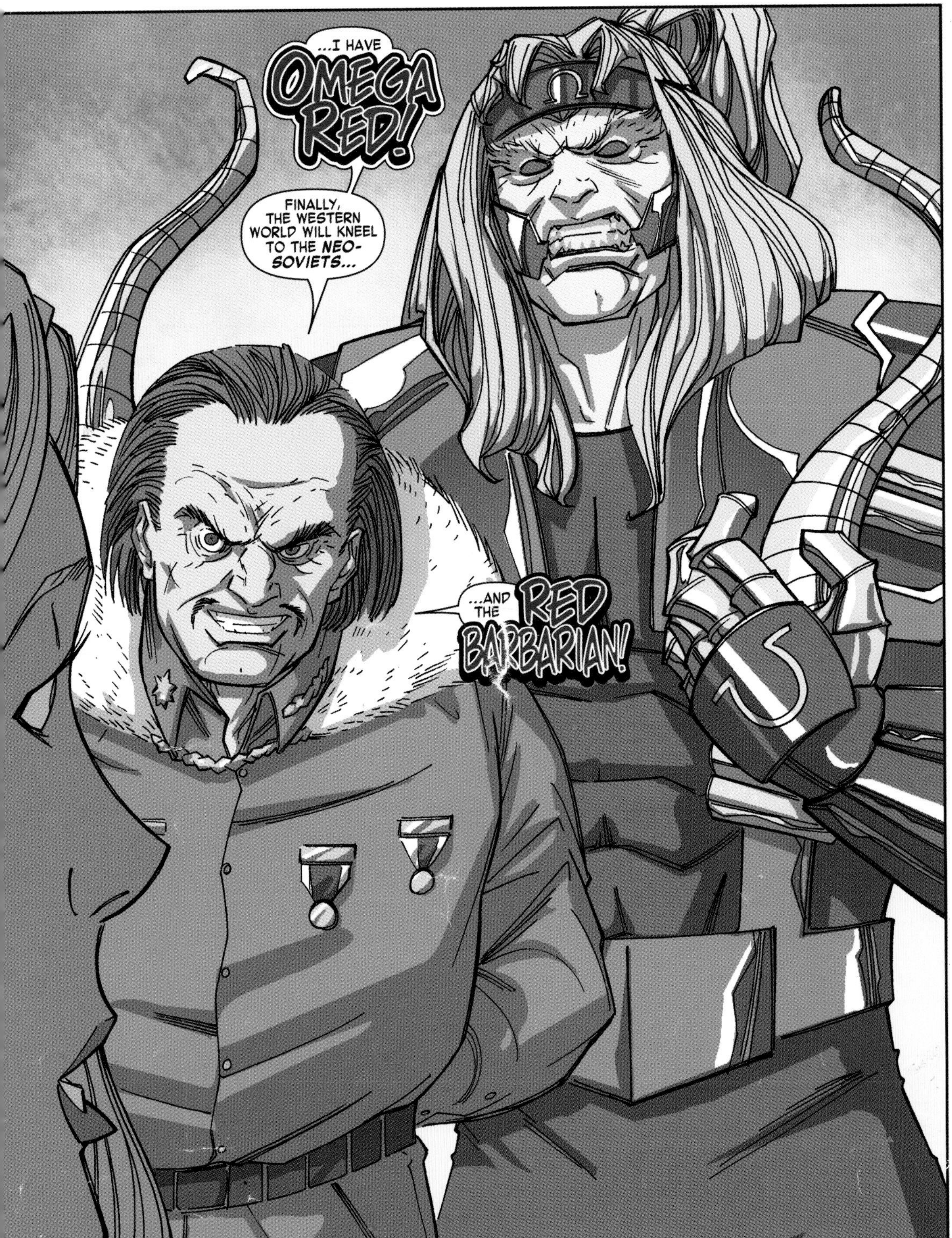

...I HAVE
OMEGA RED!
FINALLY, THE WESTERN WORLD WILL KNEEL TO THE NEO-SOVIETS...
...AND THE RED BARBARIAN!

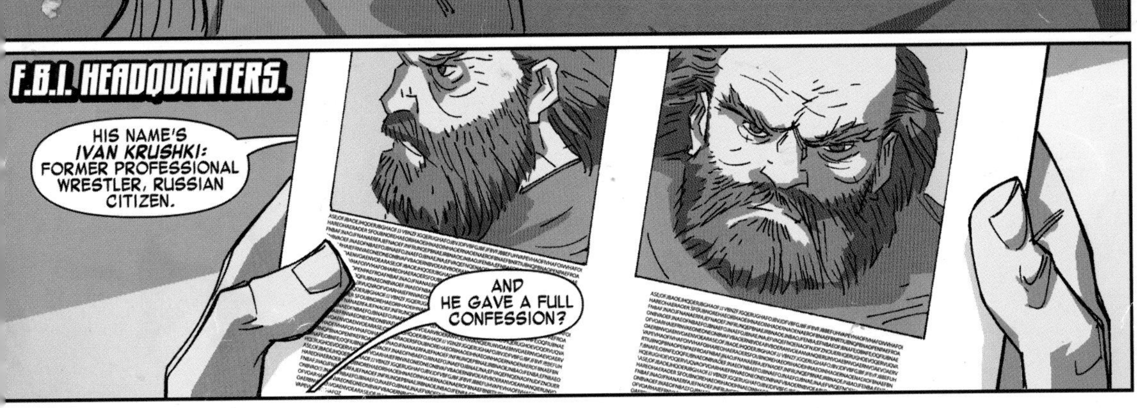

F.B.I. HEADQUARTERS.
HIS NAME'S IVAN KRUSHKI: FORMER PROFESSIONAL WRESTLER, RUSSIAN CITIZEN.
AND HE GAVE A FULL CONFESSION?

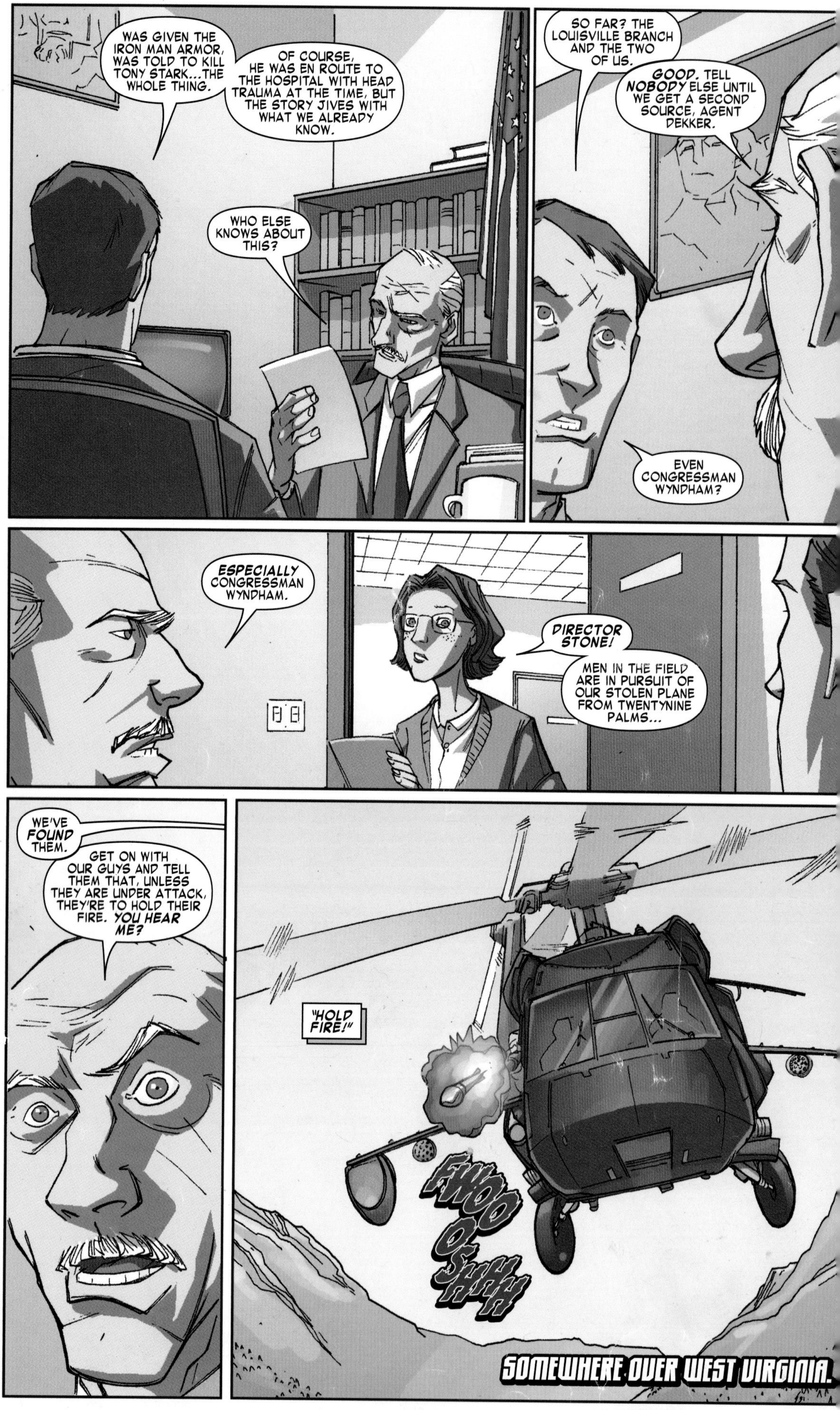
WAS GIVEN THE IRON MAN ARMOR, WAS TOLD TO KILL TONY STARK...THE WHOLE THING.
OF COURSE, HE WAS EN ROUTE TO THE HOSPITAL WITH HEAD TRAUMA AT THE TIME, BUT THE STORY JIVES WITH WHAT WE ALREADY KNOW.
WHO ELSE KNOWS ABOUT THIS?
SO FAR? THE LOUISVILLE BRANCH AND THE TWO OF US.
GOOD. TELL NOBODY ELSE UNTIL WE GET A SECOND SOURCE, AGENT DEKKER.
EVEN CONGRESSMAN WYNDHAM?
ESPECIALLY CONGRESSMAN WYNDHAM.
DIRECTOR STONE!
MEN IN THE FIELD ARE IN PURSUIT OF OUR STOLEN PLANE FROM TWENTYNINE PALMS...
WE'VE FOUND THEM.
GET ON WITH OUR GUYS AND TELL THEM THAT, UNLESS THEY ARE UNDER ATTACK, THEY'RE TO HOLD THEIR FIRE. YOU HEAR ME?
"HOLD FIRE!"
FWOOOSHHH
SOMEWHERE OVER WEST VIRGINIA.

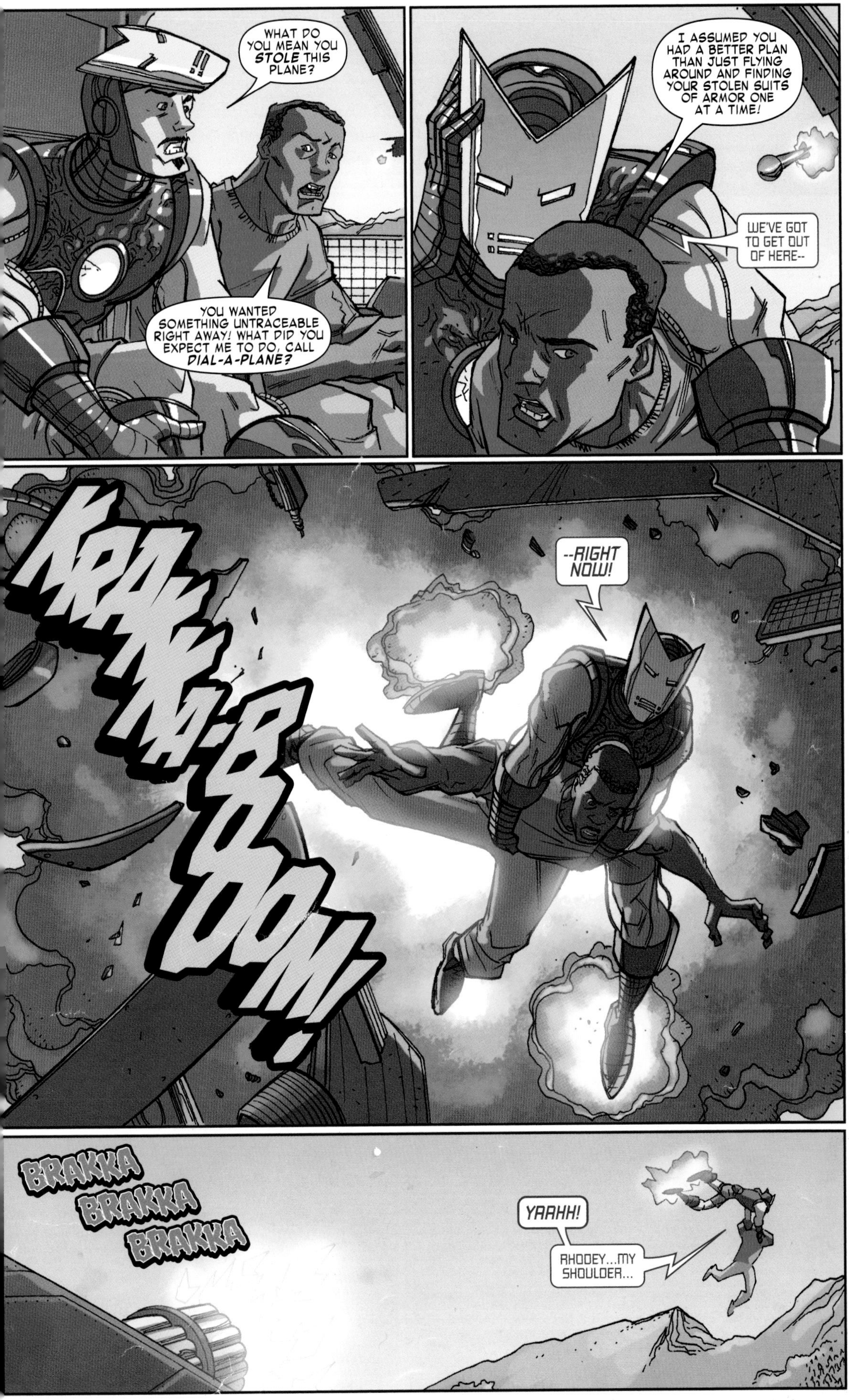
WHAT DO YOU MEAN YOU STOLE THIS PLANE?
YOU WANTED SOMETHING UNTRACEABLE RIGHT AWAY! WHAT DID YOU EXPECT ME TO DO, CALL DIAL-A-PLANE?
I ASSUMED YOU HAD A BETTER PLAN THAN JUST FLYING AROUND AND FINDING YOUR STOLEN SUITS OF ARMOR ONE AT A TIME!
WE'VE GOT TO GET OUT OF HERE--
KRAKA-BOOM!
--RIGHT NOW!
BRAKKA BRAKKA BRAKKA
YAAHH!
RHODEY...MY SHOULDER...

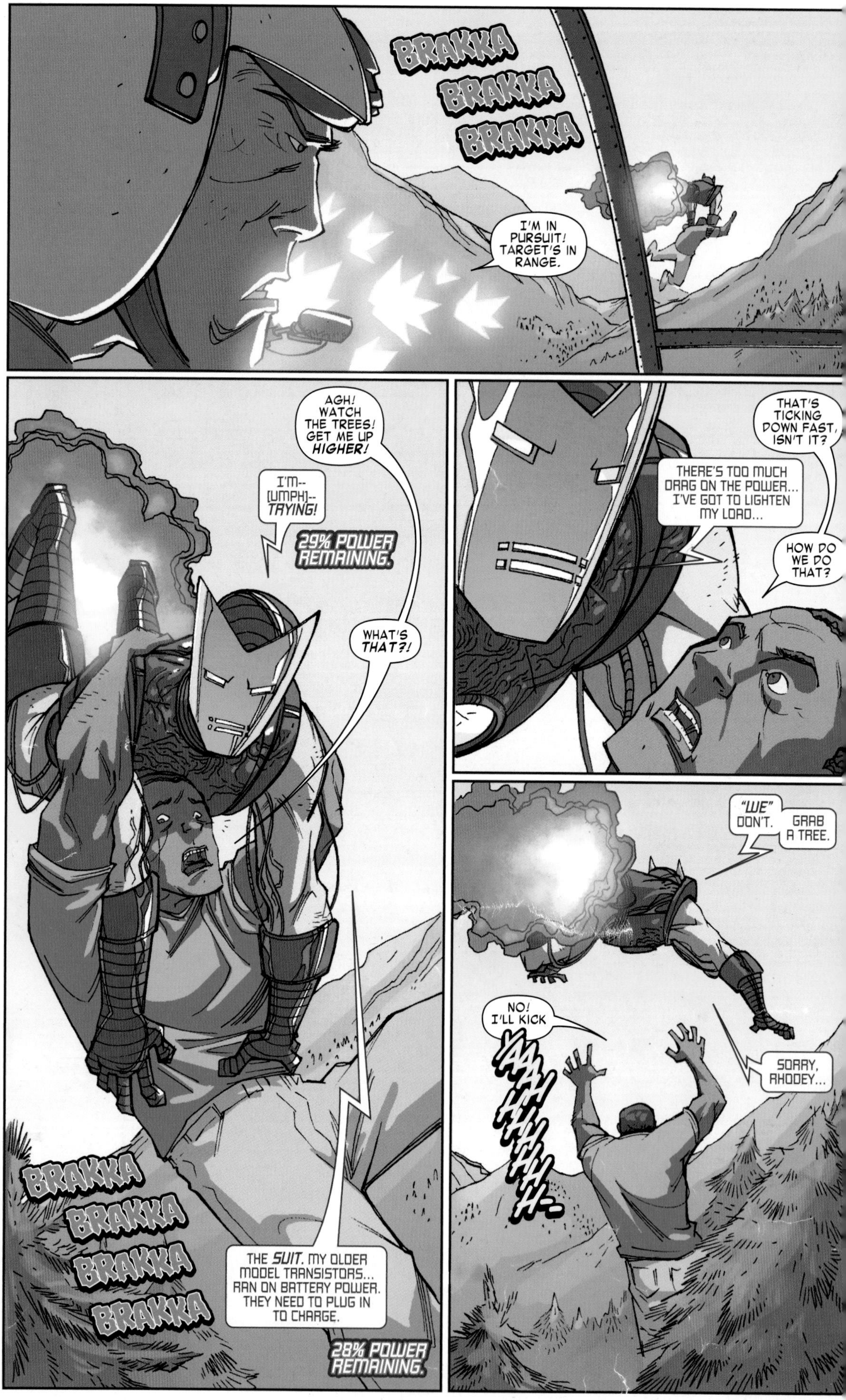
BRAKKA
BRAKKA
BRAKKA
I'M IN PURSUIT! TARGET'S IN RANGE.
AGH! WATCH THE TREES! GET ME UP HIGHER!
I'M-- [UMPH]-- TRYING!
29% POWER REMAINING.
WHAT'S THAT?!
THE SUIT. MY OLDER MODEL TRANSISTORS... RAN ON BATTERY POWER. THEY NEED TO PLUG IN TO CHARGE.
BRAKKA
BRAKKA
BRAKKA
BRAKKA
28% POWER REMAINING.
THAT'S TICKING DOWN FAST, ISN'T IT?
THERE'S TOO MUCH DRAG ON THE POWER... I'VE GOT TO LIGHTEN MY LOAD...
HOW DO WE DO THAT?
"WE" DON'T.
GRAB A TREE.
NO! I'LL KICK
YAAAHHHHHHHH-
SORRY, RHODEY...

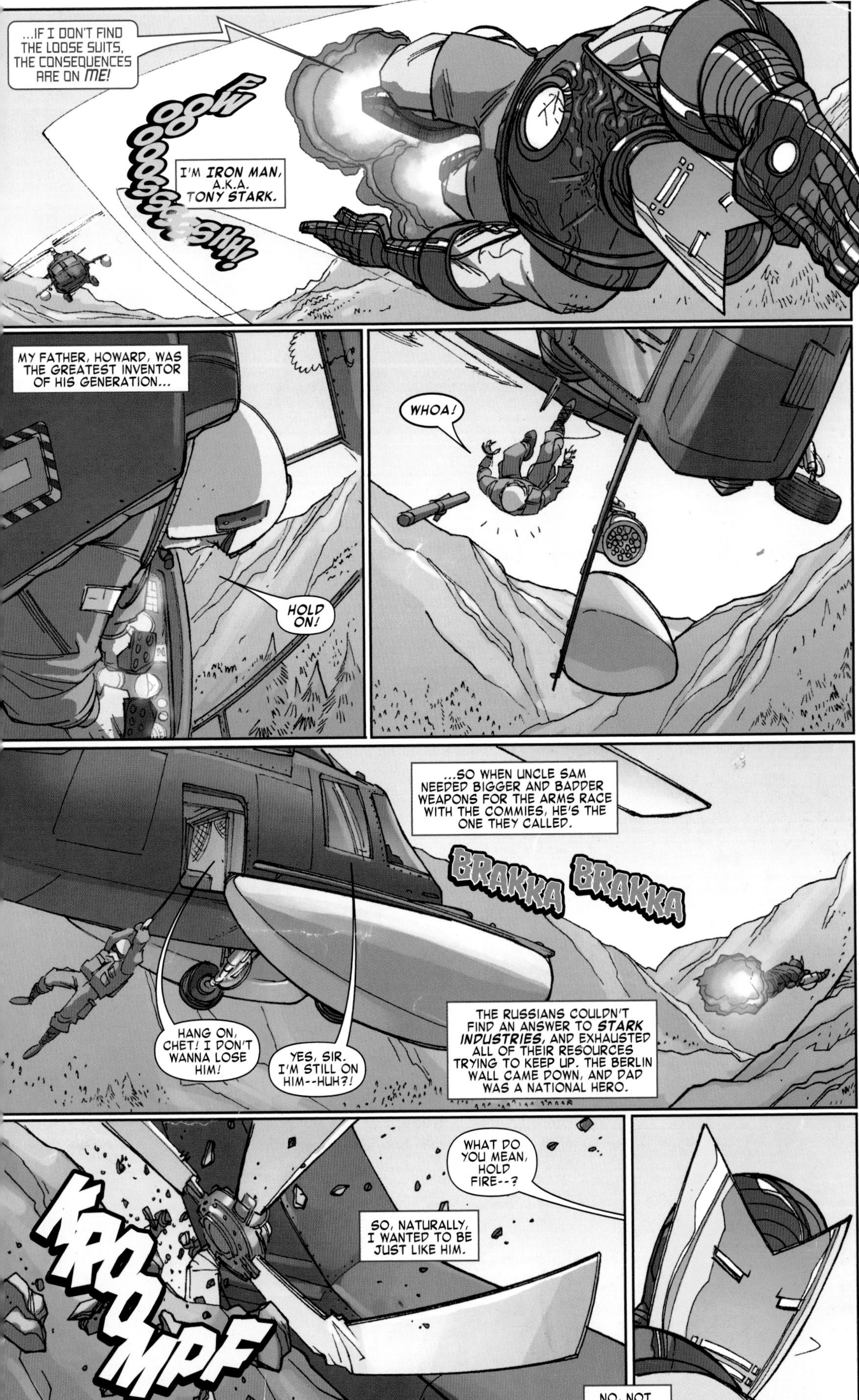
...IF I DON'T FIND THE LOOSE SUITS, THE CONSEQUENCES ARE ON *ME!*
FOOOOOOOSSSSSHH!
I'M **IRON MAN**, A.K.A. TONY **STARK.**
MY FATHER, HOWARD, WAS THE GREATEST INVENTOR OF HIS GENERATION...
HOLD ON!
WHOA!
...SO WHEN UNCLE SAM NEEDED BIGGER AND BADDER WEAPONS FOR THE ARMS RACE WITH THE COMMIES, HE'S THE ONE THEY CALLED.
BRAKKA BRAKKA
HANG ON, CHET! I DON'T WANNA LOSE HIM!
YES, SIR. I'M STILL ON HIM--HUH?!
THE RUSSIANS COULDN'T FIND AN ANSWER TO **STARK INDUSTRIES,** AND EXHAUSTED ALL OF THEIR RESOURCES TRYING TO KEEP UP. THE BERLIN WALL CAME DOWN, AND DAD WAS A NATIONAL HERO.
KROOMPF
SO, NATURALLY, I WANTED TO BE JUST LIKE HIM.
WHAT DO YOU MEAN, HOLD FIRE--?
NO, NOT *"LIKE"* HIM...

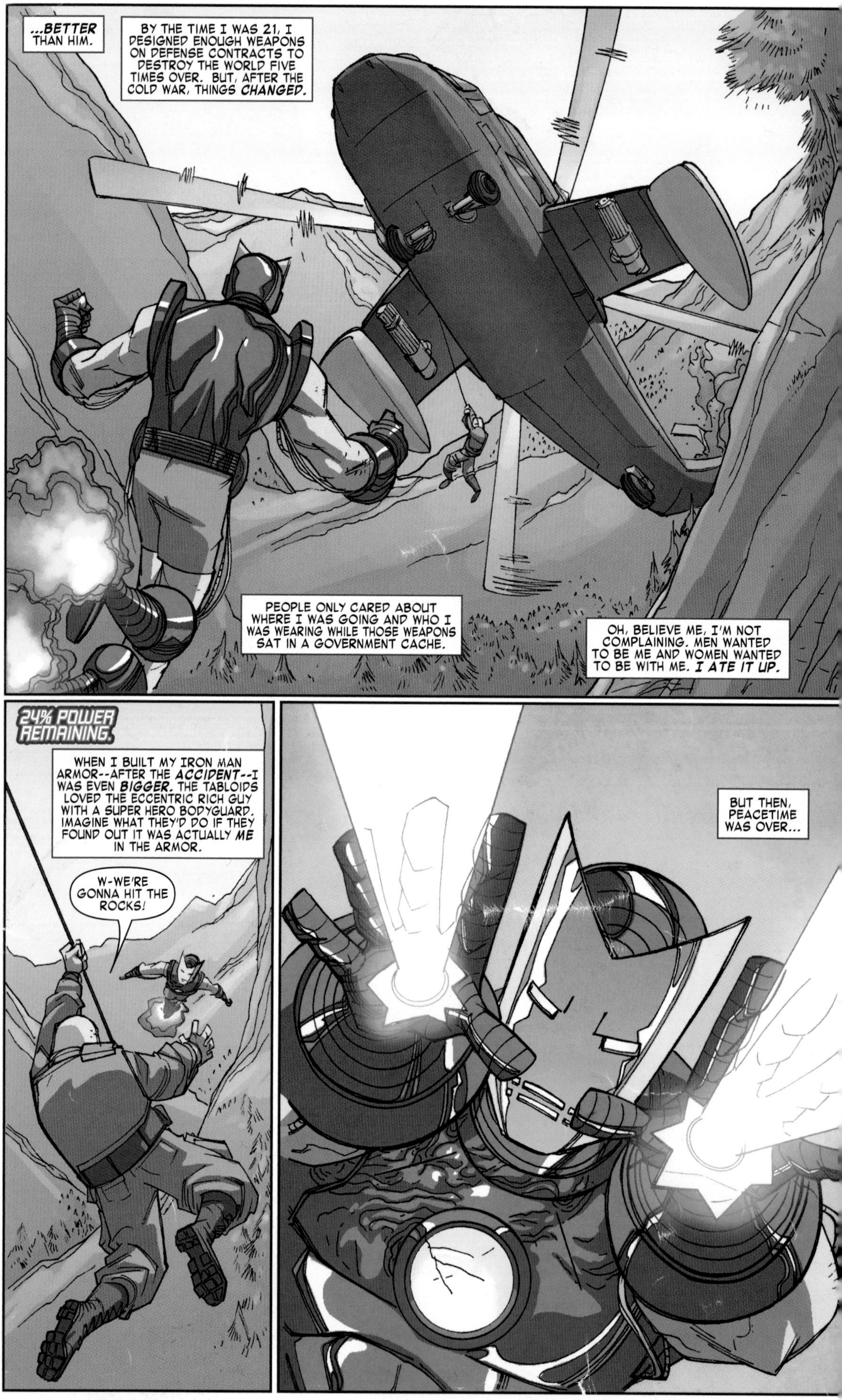
...BETTER THAN HIM.
BY THE TIME I WAS 21, I DESIGNED ENOUGH WEAPONS ON DEFENSE CONTRACTS TO DESTROY THE WORLD FIVE TIMES OVER. BUT, AFTER THE COLD WAR, THINGS CHANGED.
PEOPLE ONLY CARED ABOUT WHERE I WAS GOING AND WHO I WAS WEARING WHILE THOSE WEAPONS SAT IN A GOVERNMENT CACHE.
OH, BELIEVE ME, I'M NOT COMPLAINING. MEN WANTED TO BE ME AND WOMEN WANTED TO BE WITH ME. I ATE IT UP.
24% POWER REMAINING.
WHEN I BUILT MY IRON MAN ARMOR--AFTER THE ACCIDENT--I WAS EVEN BIGGER. THE TABLOIDS LOVED THE ECCENTRIC RICH GUY WITH A SUPER HERO BODYGUARD. IMAGINE WHAT THEY'D DO IF THEY FOUND OUT IT WAS ACTUALLY ME IN THE ARMOR.
W-WE'RE GONNA HIT THE ROCKS!
BUT THEN, PEACETIME WAS OVER...

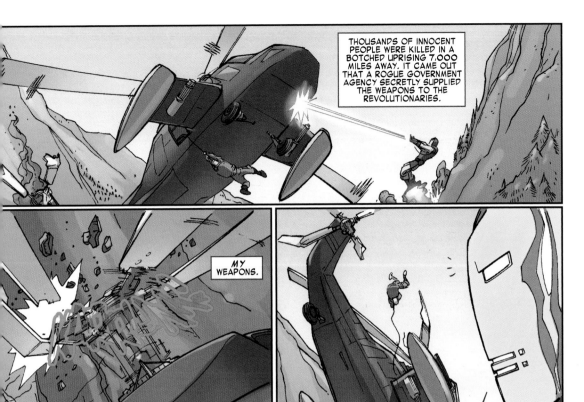

THOUSANDS OF INNOCENT PEOPLE WERE KILLED IN A BOTCHED UPRISING 7,000 MILES AWAY. IT CAME OUT THAT A ROGUE GOVERNMENT AGENCY SECRETLY SUPPLIED THE WEAPONS TO THE REVOLUTIONARIES.

MY WEAPONS.

AMERICANS FELT BETRAYED. THEY CALLED ME A KILLER. I WASN'T A *KEEPER* OF THE *PEACE* ANYMORE, I WAS A *MERCHANT* OF *DEATH*.

21% POWER REMAINING.

SO I CLOSED UP SHOP AND VOWED TO NEVER MAKE WEAPONS AGAIN. I OPENED A NEW COMPANY, STARK *ENTERPRISES*, AS FAR AWAY FROM NEW YORK AS I COULD GET.

HOLLYWOOD WAS A PLACE WHERE I COULD BE LOVED JUST BECAUSE I'M FAMOUS.

IT'S WORKED FOR A WHILE--

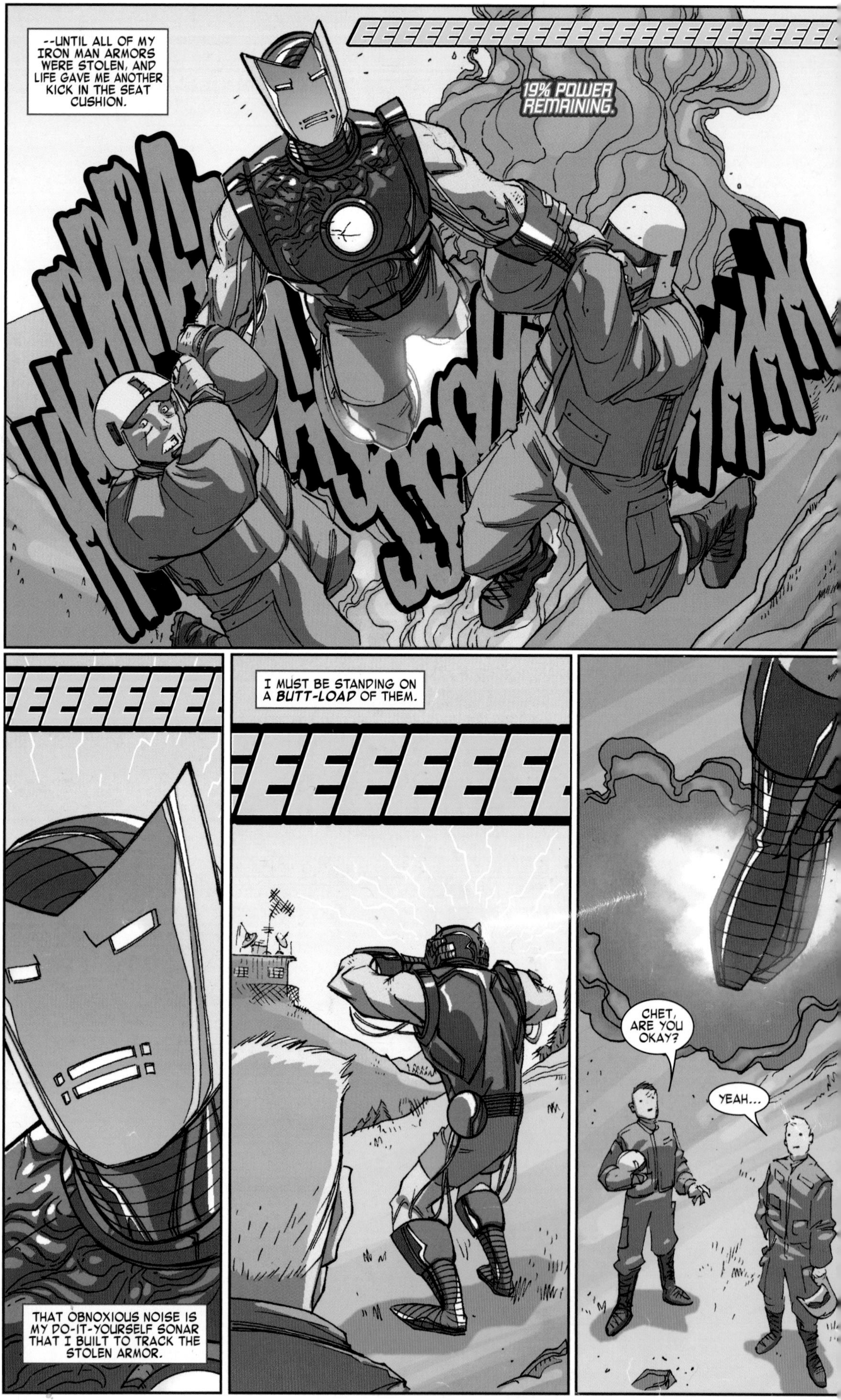
--UNTIL ALL OF MY IRON MAN ARMORS WERE STOLEN, AND LIFE GAVE ME ANOTHER KICK IN THE SEAT CUSHION.
EEEEEEEEEEEEEEEEEEEEEEEE
19% POWER REMAINING.
EEEEEEEE
THAT OBNOXIOUS NOISE IS MY DO-IT-YOURSELF SONAR THAT I BUILT TO TRACK THE STOLEN ARMOR.
I MUST BE STANDING ON A *BUTT-LOAD* OF THEM.
EEEEEEEE
CHET, ARE YOU OKAY?
YEAH...

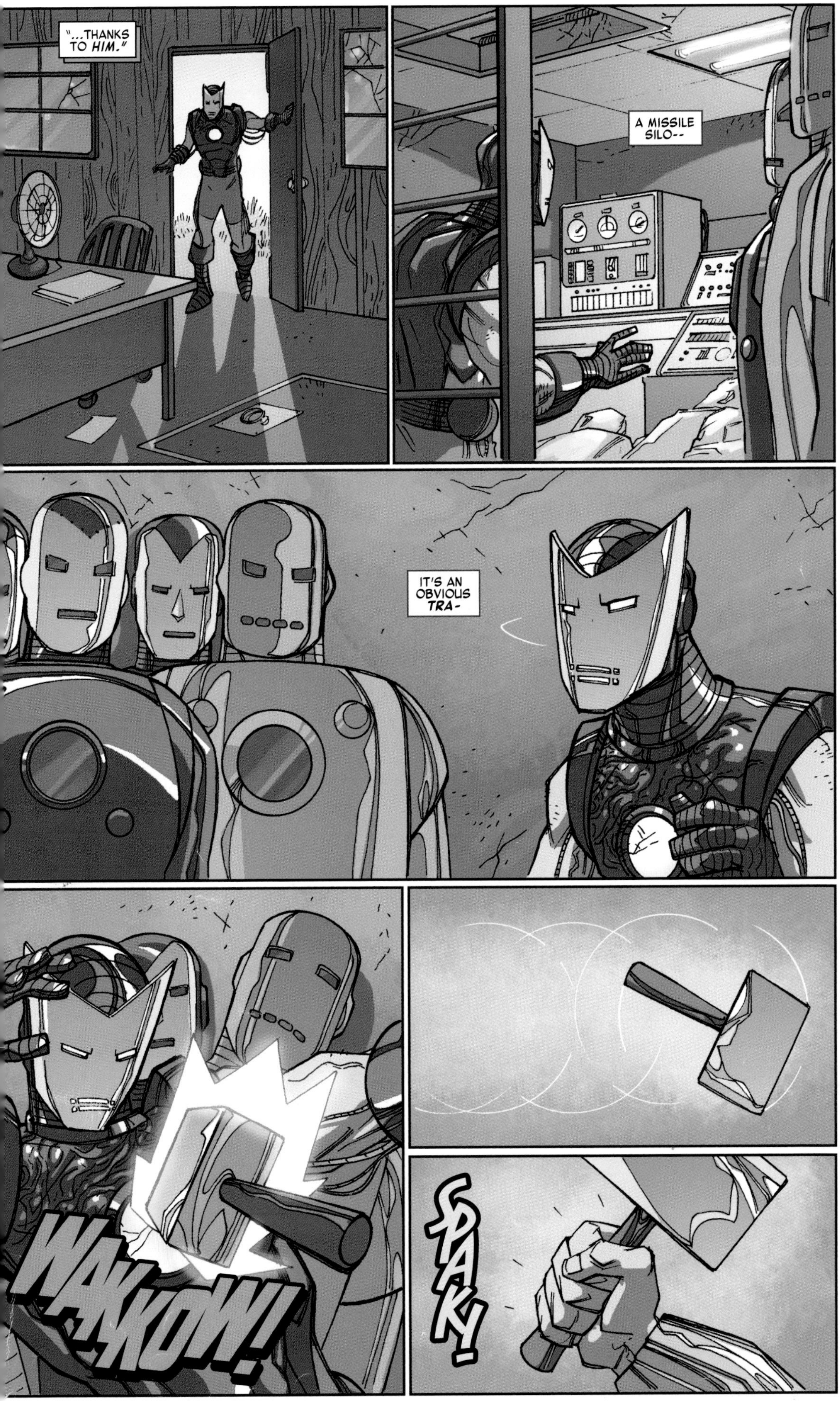
"...THANKS TO HIM."
A MISSILE SILO--
IT'S AN OBVIOUS TRA-
WAKKOW!
SPAK!

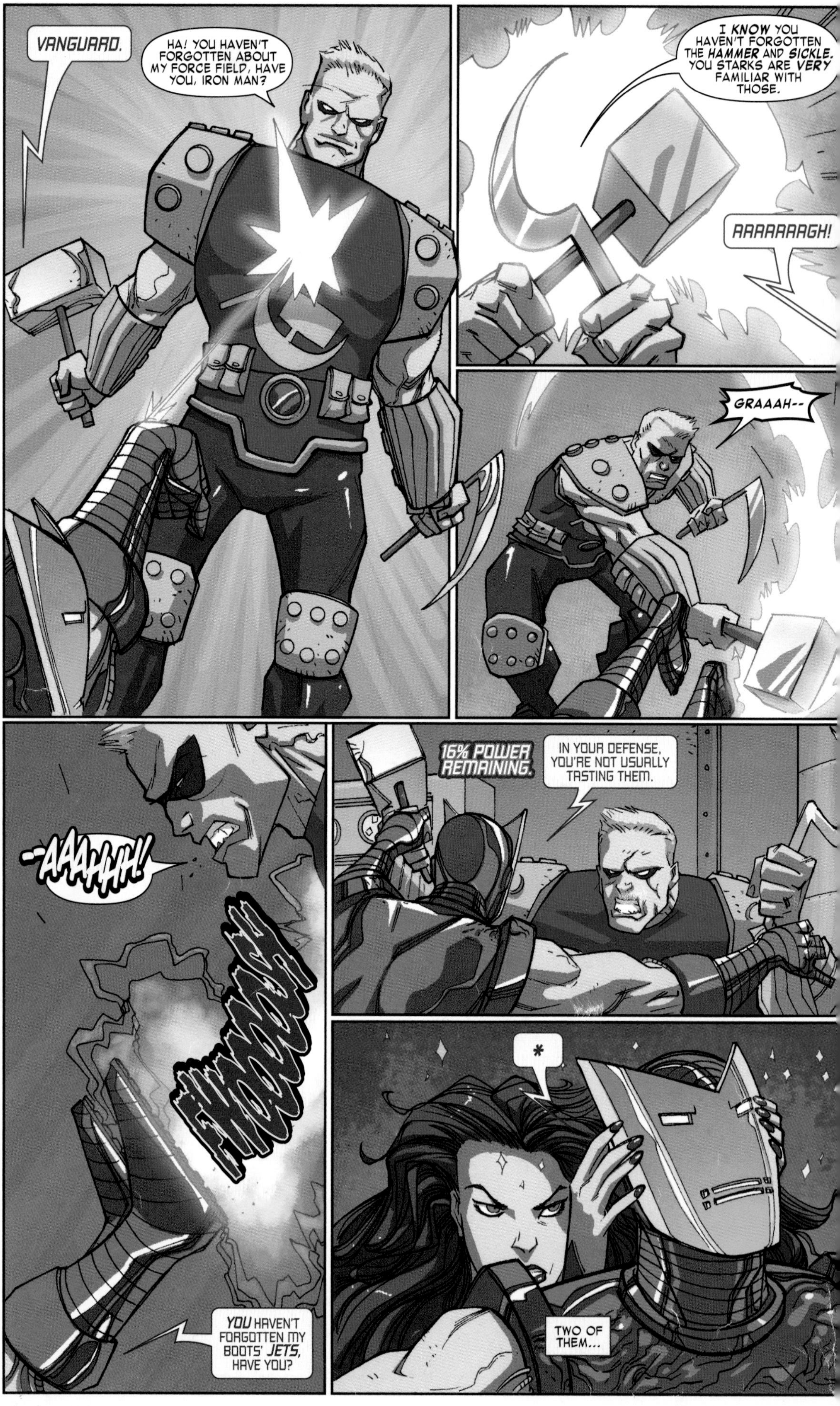
VANGUARD.
HA! YOU HAVEN'T FORGOTTEN ABOUT MY FORCE FIELD, HAVE YOU, IRON MAN?
I KNOW YOU HAVEN'T FORGOTTEN THE HAMMER AND SICKLE. YOU STARKS ARE VERY FAMILIAR WITH THOSE.
AAAAAAAGH!
GRAAAH--
--AAAHHH!
FWOOOSH
YOU HAVEN'T FORGOTTEN MY BOOTS' JETS, HAVE YOU?
16% POWER REMAINING.
IN YOUR DEFENSE, YOU'RE NOT USUALLY TASTING THEM.
*
TWO OF THEM...

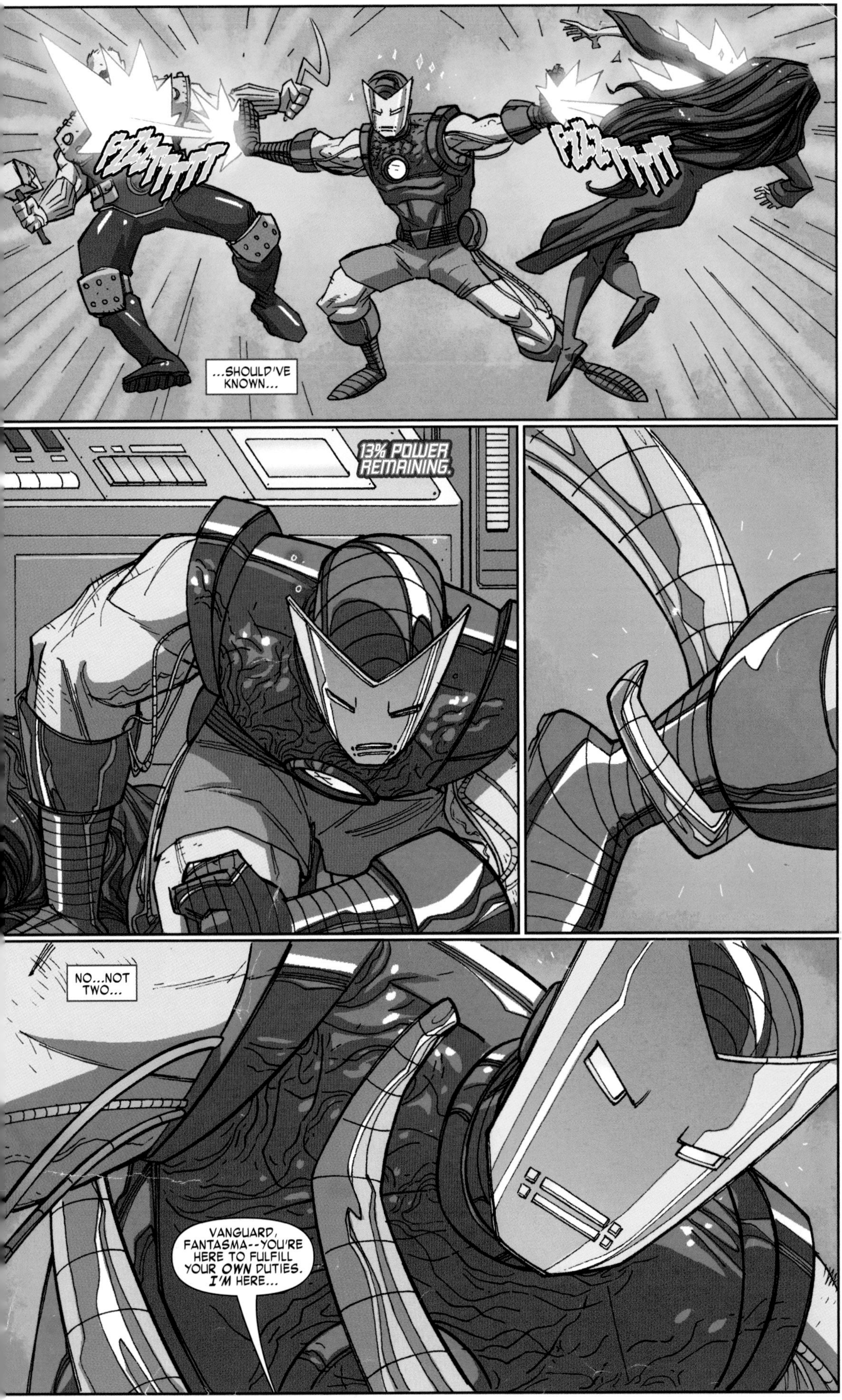
FZZZTTTTTT
FZZZTTTTTT
...SHOULD'VE KNOWN...
13% POWER REMAINING.
NO...NOT TWO...
VANGUARD, FANTASMA--YOU'RE HERE TO FULFILL YOUR OWN DUTIES. I'M HERE...

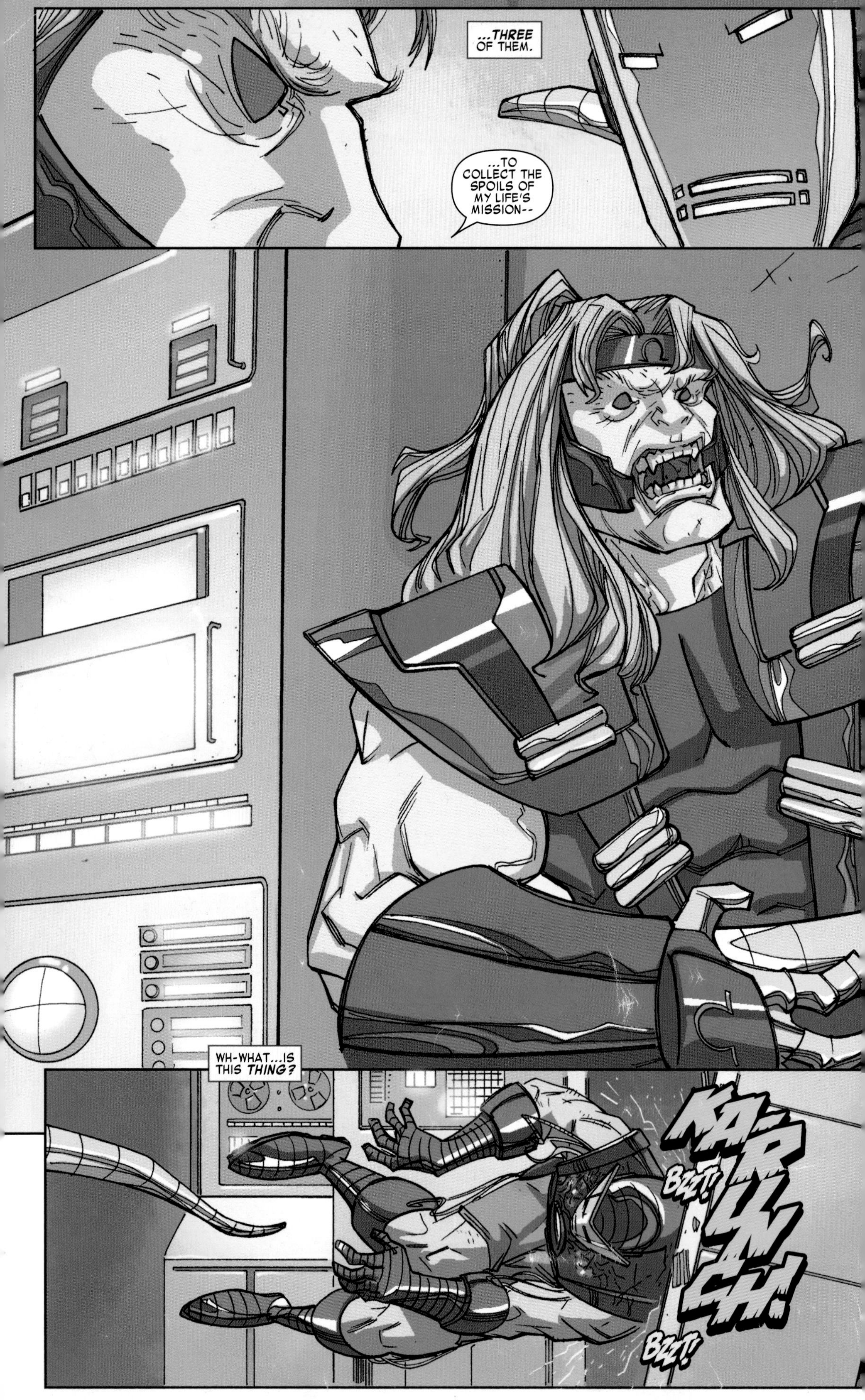
...THREE OF THEM.
...TO COLLECT THE SPOILS OF MY LIFE'S MISSION--
WH-WHAT...IS THIS THING?
KA-RUNCH!
BZZT!
BZZT!

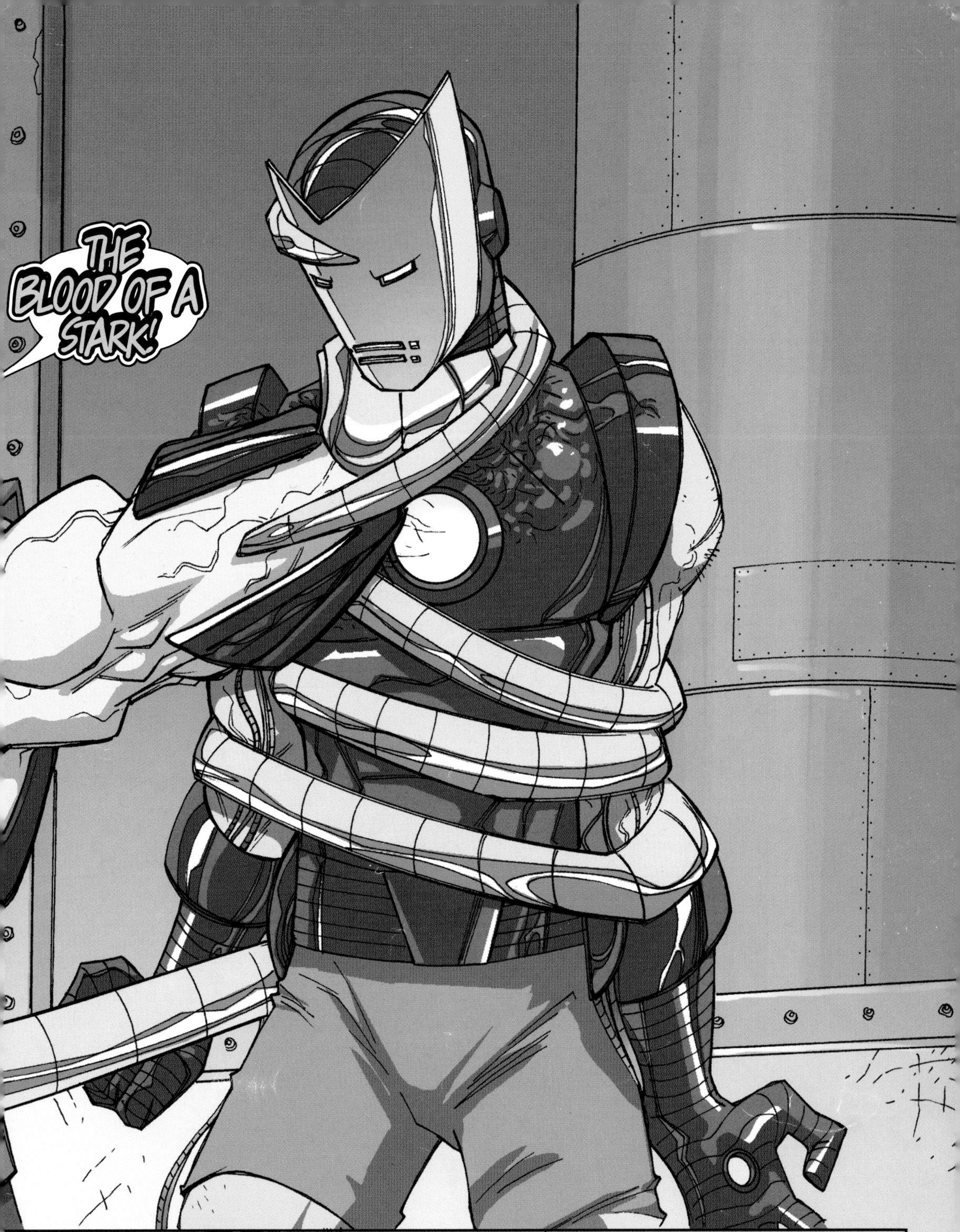
THE BLOOD OF A STARK!

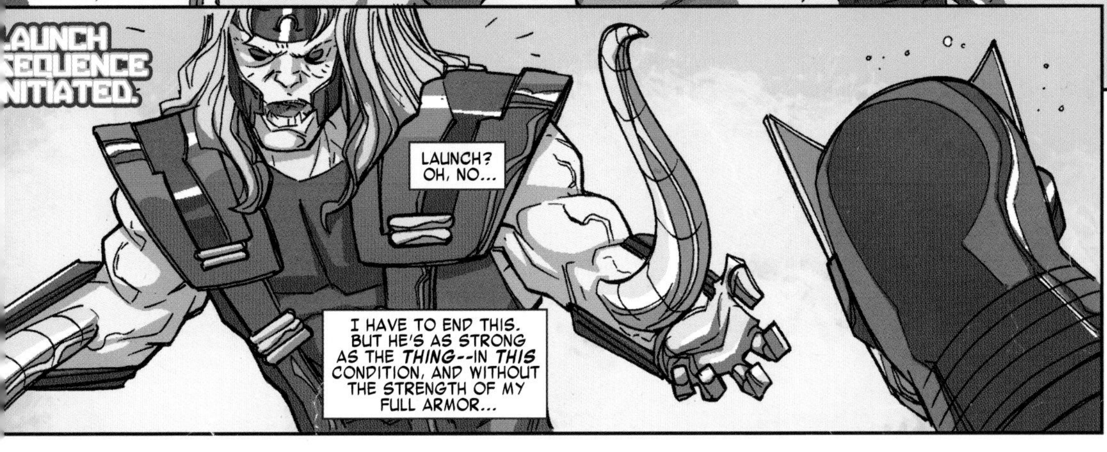
LAUNCH SEQUENCE INITIATED.
LAUNCH? OH, NO...
I HAVE TO END THIS. BUT HE'S AS STRONG AS THE *THING*--IN *THIS* CONDITION, AND WITHOUT THE STRENGTH OF MY FULL ARMOR...

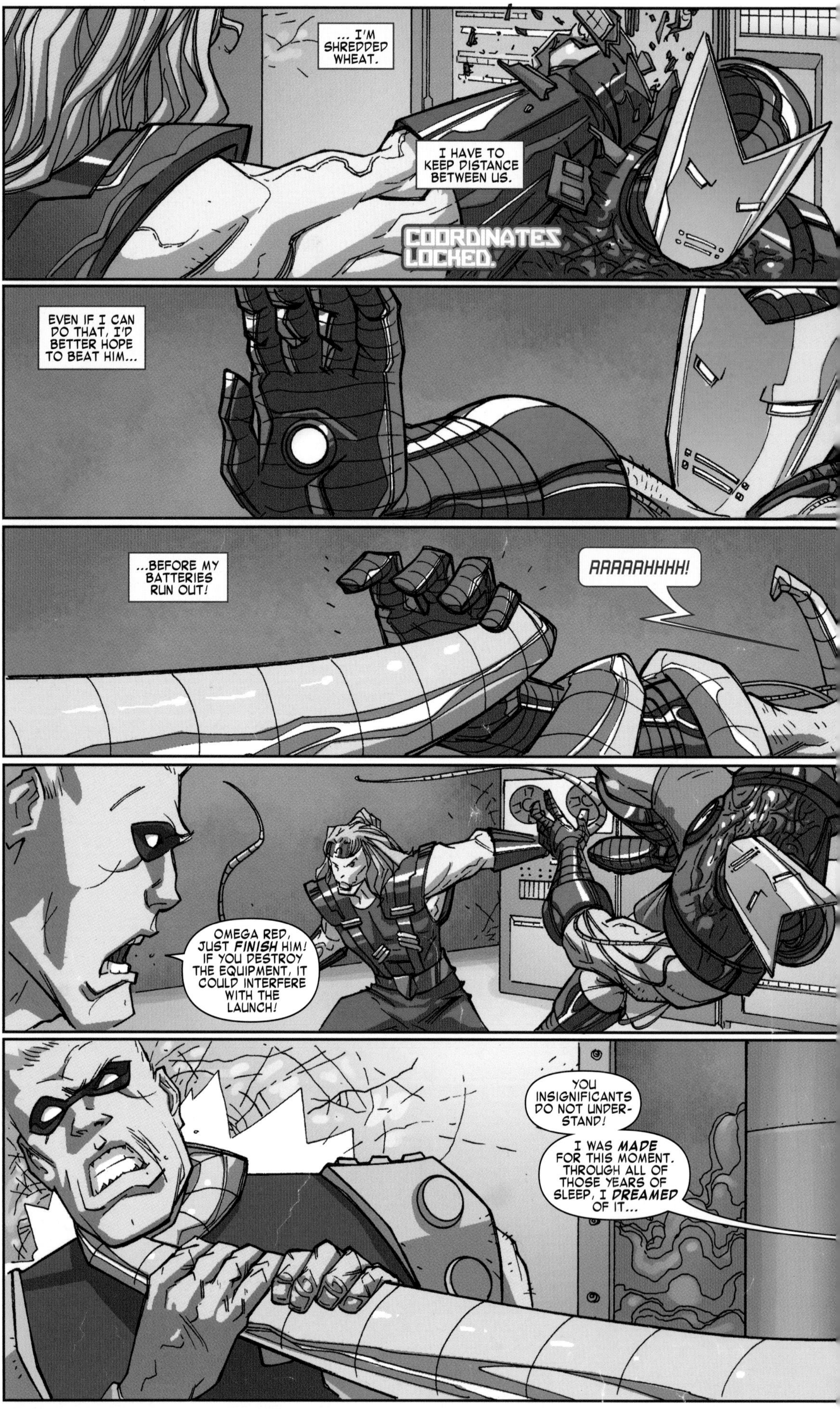

... I'M SHREDDED WHEAT.
I HAVE TO KEEP DISTANCE BETWEEN US.
COORDINATES LOCKED.
EVEN IF I CAN DO THAT, I'D BETTER HOPE TO BEAT HIM...
...BEFORE MY BATTERIES RUN OUT!
AAAAAHHHH!
OMEGA RED, JUST *FINISH* HIM! IF YOU DESTROY THE EQUIPMENT, IT COULD INTERFERE WITH THE LAUNCH!
YOU INSIGNIFICANTS DO NOT UNDER-STAND!
I WAS *MADE* FOR THIS MOMENT. THROUGH ALL OF THOSE YEARS OF SLEEP, I *DREAMED* OF IT...

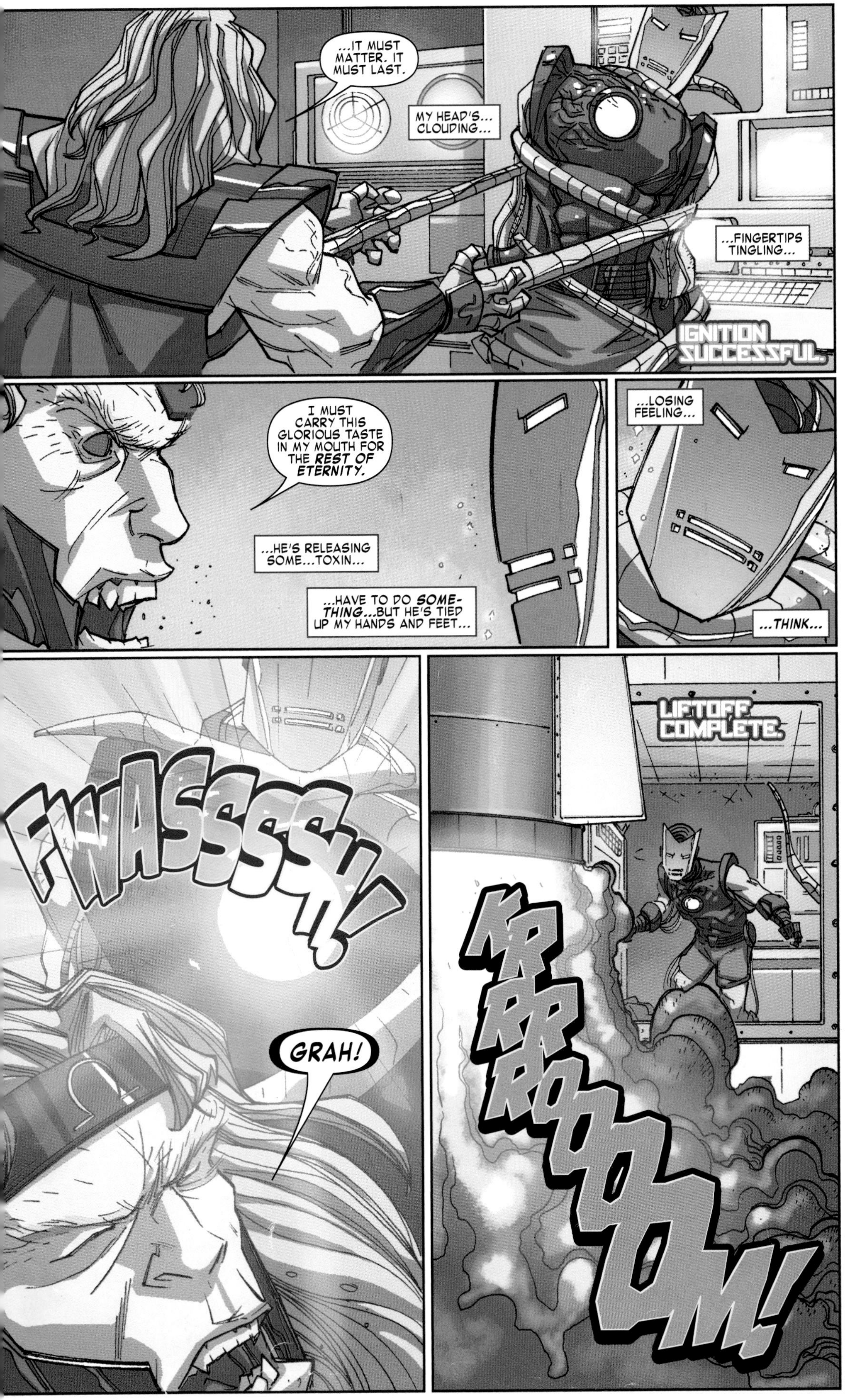
...IT MUST MATTER. IT MUST LAST.
MY HEAD'S... CLOUDING...
...FINGERTIPS TINGLING...
IGNITION SUCCESSFUL.
I MUST CARRY THIS GLORIOUS TASTE IN MY MOUTH FOR THE REST OF ETERNITY.
...HE'S RELEASING SOME...TOXIN...
...HAVE TO DO SOMETHING...BUT HE'S TIED UP MY HANDS AND FEET...
...LOSING FEELING...
...THINK...
FWASSSSH!
GRAH!
LIFTOFF COMPLETE.
KRRRRROOOOOOM!

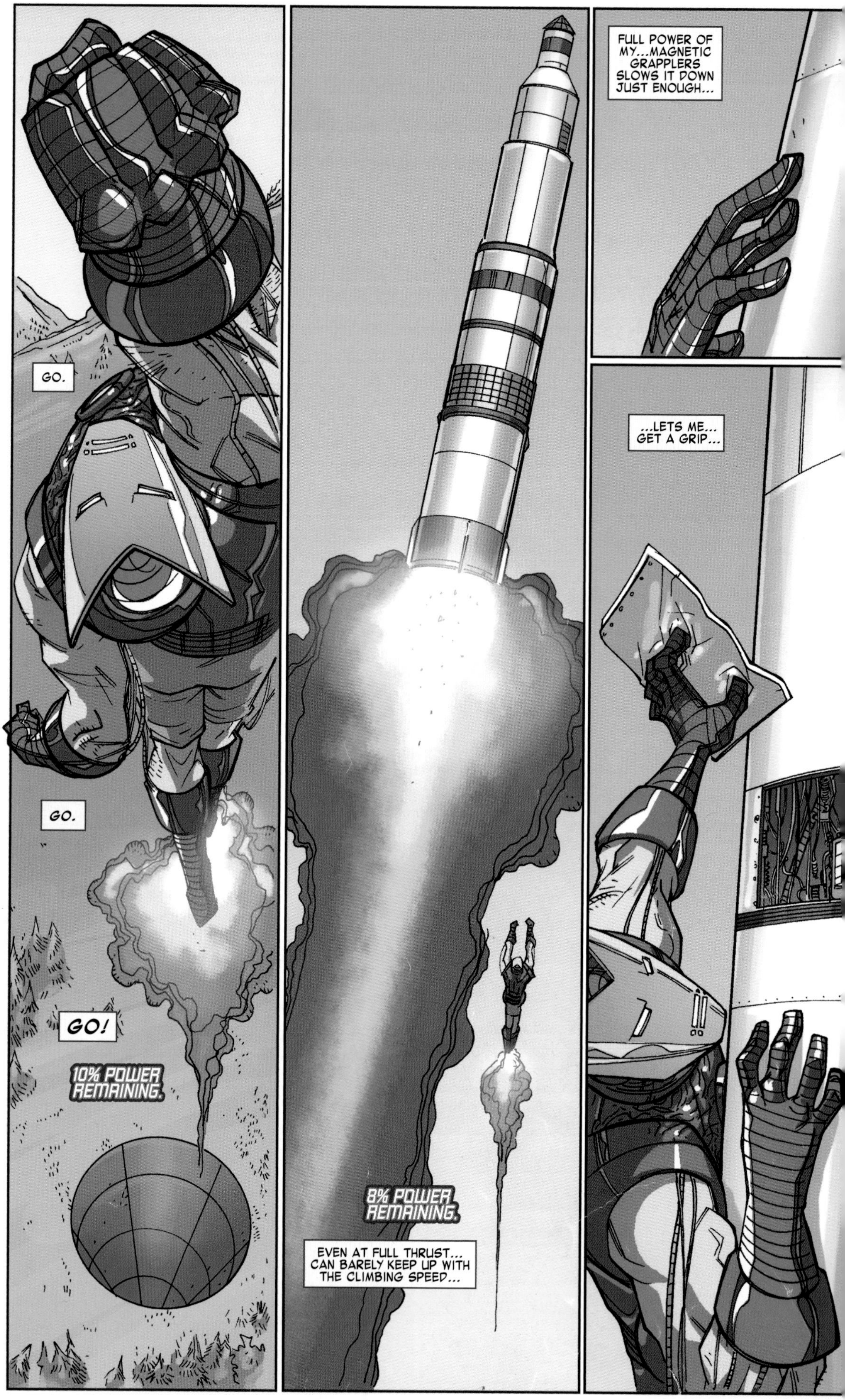
GO.
GO.
GO!
10% POWER REMAINING.
8% POWER REMAINING.
EVEN AT FULL THRUST... CAN BARELY KEEP UP WITH THE CLIMBING SPEED...
FULL POWER OF MY...MAGNETIC GRAPPLERS SLOWS IT DOWN JUST ENOUGH...
...LETS ME... GET A GRIP...

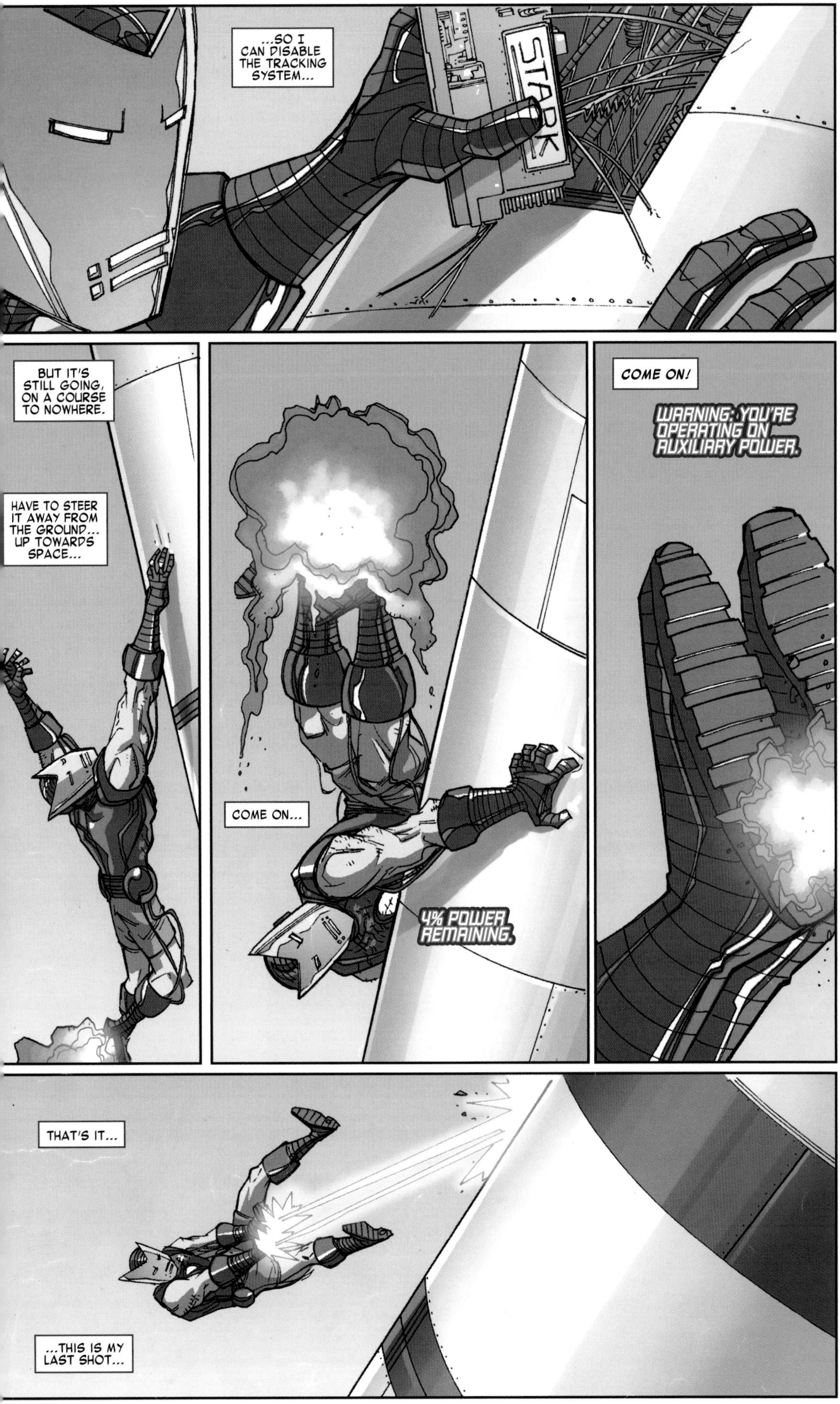
...SO I CAN DISABLE THE TRACKING SYSTEM...
BUT IT'S STILL GOING, ON A COURSE TO NOWHERE.
HAVE TO STEER IT AWAY FROM THE GROUND... UP TOWARDS SPACE...
COME ON...
4% POWER REMAINING.
COME ON!
WARNING: YOU'RE OPERATING ON AUXILIARY POWER.
THAT'S IT...
...THIS IS MY LAST SHOT...

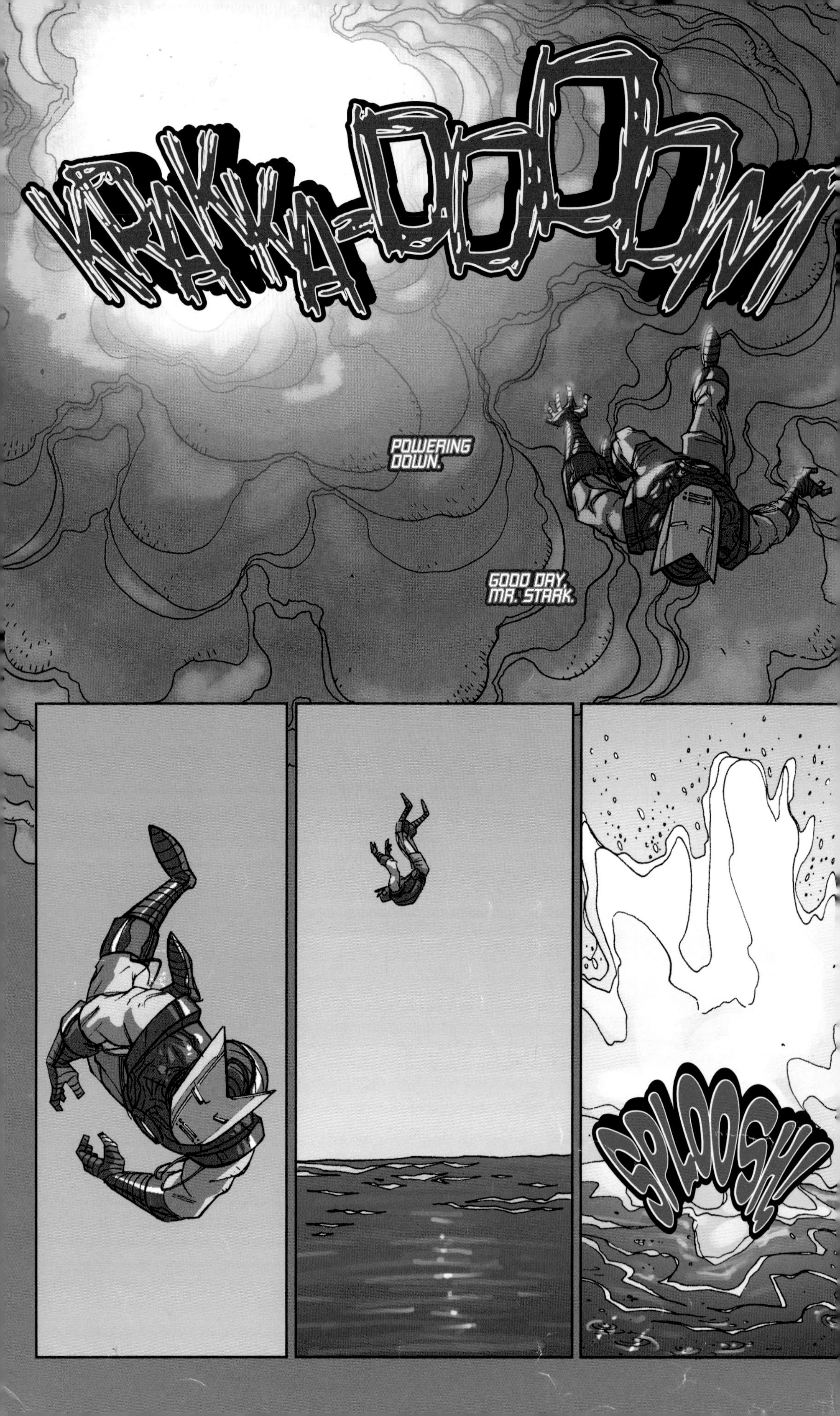
KRAKKA-DOOOOM!
POWERING DOWN.
GOOD DAY, MR. STARK.
SPLOOSH!

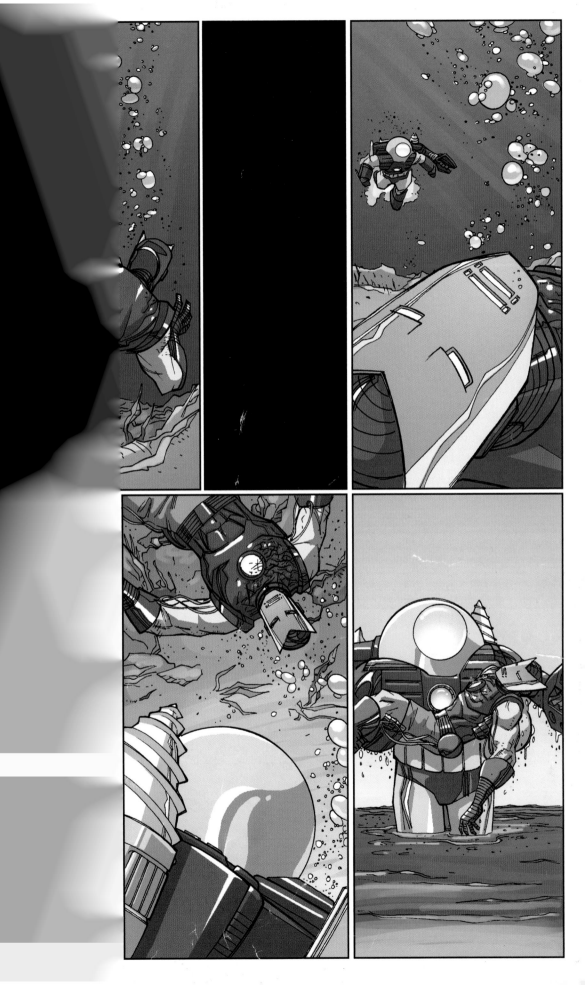

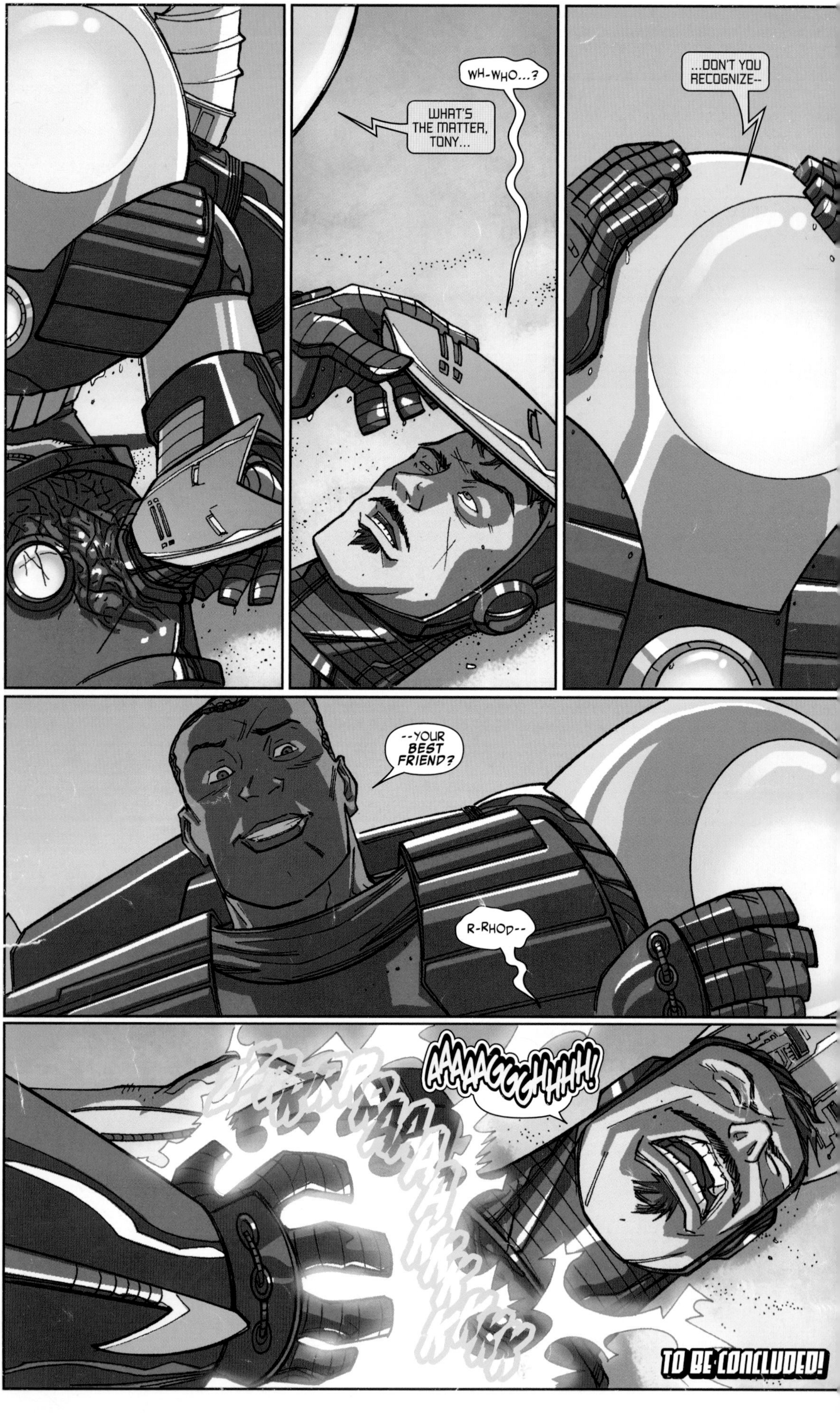
WH-WHO...?
WHAT'S THE MATTER, TONY...
...DON'T YOU RECOGNIZE--
--YOUR BEST FRIEND?
R-RHOD--
AAAAAGGHHHH!
TO BE CONCLUDED!